MW00886873

The GO AWAYS

TAMI HICKS
ILLUSTRATIONS BY ALLA VASILENKO

ISBN: 9781735337319 Paperback
ISBN: 9781735337302 Hardcover

Dedicated to

My Mom

Who always sees the best in me. Through my failures and successes, you have always believed in me, supported me, been my voice of reason, and my biggest encouragement. Thank you, Mary Hicks, for being you.

It was a beautiful sunny afternoon as the clouds changed themselves into animals for the kids to find. They loved to see the kids laugh.

"Oh, look a giraffe!" said the girl.

"And I see a snail!" said the boy.

RC had been watching from a distance. *Maybe it will work this time*, he thought, as he slowly floated over to the kids. He thought very hard about what he would change into.

A dog! he thought. *Kids love dogs!*

As RC floated above the kids to change into a dog, the other clouds saw RC coming towards them. They cried out, "RC, *noooooo!*"

But, RC had already started to rain, just like he always did, and the kids ran away just like they always did.

The other clouds yelled at RC. “You always ruin it! GO AWAY!”

RC was so distracted by the faces the other clouds were making at him, he didn’t notice the strong wind until it was too late.

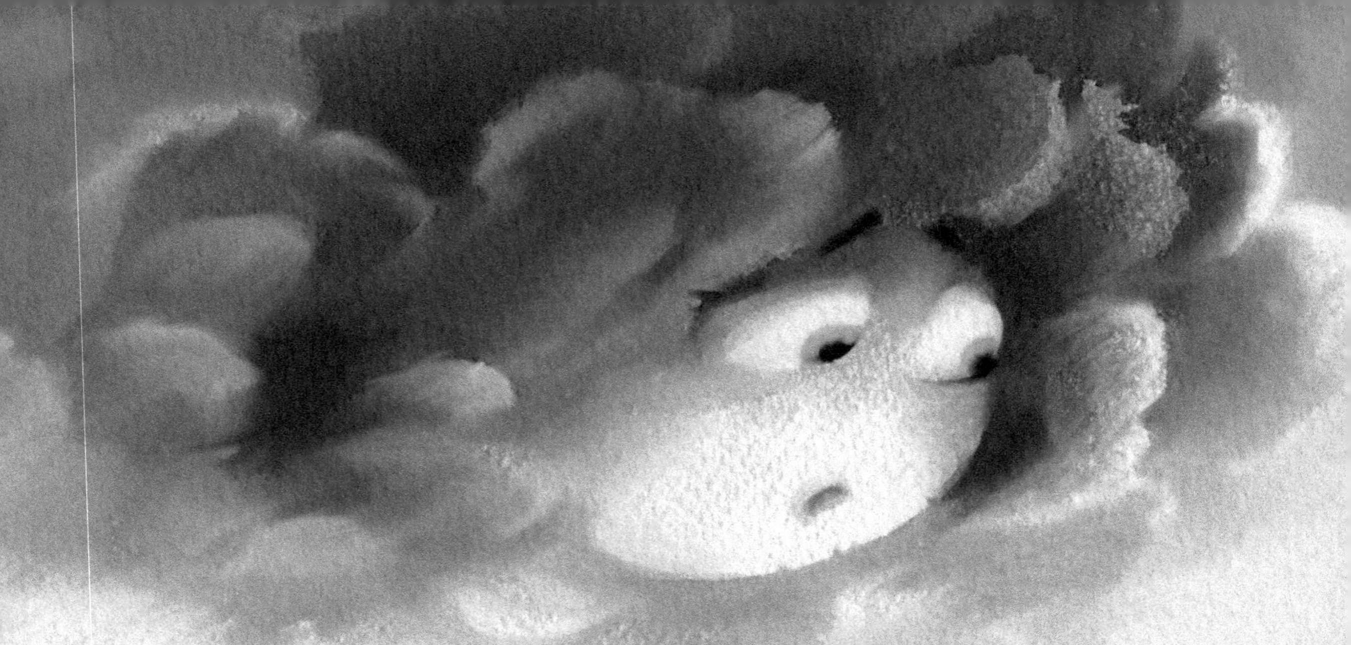

The wind blew and blew and tossed RC all around. Then finally, the wind stopped.

"Where am I?" he asked, expecting no one to answer.

But a voice did answer. "You are in the desert of GO AWAY."

"What is the desert of GO AWAY? I have never heard of it," he asked the faceless voice.

"It is a place where the wind brings you when you are yelled at to GO AWAY!" said a chameleon jumping up from under the sand. "Hi, my name is Scoot."

"Hi, Scoot, my name is RC. I thought chameleons were supposed to blend into their surroundings," RC inquired.

Scoot answered sadly, "I was born this color. That is why I am here in GO AWAY."

"Every time my friends and I would go out to catch bugs, the bugs would always see us coming because I couldn't change colors and blend in. So, they would get away. One day, everyone had enough and yelled at me to GO AWAY! Then this strong wind came out of nowhere and dropped me here."

"GO AWAY! That's what the other clouds yelled at me," said RC. "I thought I was the only one who ruined things for my friends."

"Oh no," said Scoot. "There are others here besides me."

RC was scared but he was also hopeful that this might be a place where he would not be yelled at anymore.

"Where are they?" asked RC "I would like to meet them."

"They are in town," answered Scoot. "I know they would like to meet you too."

So, RC followed Scoot.

Just as they got to the town the others came out of their forts.

"Hey everyone, this is RC. The wind brought him here too!" said Scoot. "RC, meet the Go Aways."

"Hey!" said the hedgehog. "My name is Potato. The wind brought me here because when we were hibernating, I would keep everyone awake. I have too many eyes and I can't keep all of them closed at the same time, so I can't sleep long enough to hibernate. Everyone got mad at me and yelled at me to GO AWAY so they could sleep. When I walked out of the den this strong wind came out of nowhere and dropped me here."

“Hi!” said the fox. “My name is Pip. I’m here because one of my ears is smaller than the other and I couldn’t hear when the man came out of his house to chase us away from his crops. We barely escaped. The other foxes were so mad they yelled at me to GO AWAY! Then this strong wind came out of nowhere and dropped me here.”

“Hello,” said the cheetah. “My name is Dilly. “When I and the other cheetahs would race, I was too slow and took too long to catch up with them. They got tired of waiting for me to play the next game, so they yelled at me to GO AWAY and left without me. Then this strong wind came out of nowhere and dropped me here.”

“Nice to meet you,” called a voice from the sky. “My name is Squawk,” said the raven as she landed.

“I’m here because my caw is so loud that I annoyed everyone. So, they all yelled at me to GO AWAY! Then this strong wind came out of nowhere and dropped me here.”

“Nice to meet all of you,” said RC. “I was yelled at to GO AWAY because every time I tried to change into an animal to make the kids laugh, I would rain on them and ruin their sunny day and they would run away.”

“Can you change into an animal for us?” asked Scoot.

RC changed into a dog and started raining. He expected to be yelled at, but they were all laughing and running to jump in the puddle he had made.

“That was so cool!” said Pip.

“So awesome,” said Potato, as he rolled around in the puddle.

RC had this sudden fluttery feeling he had never felt before.

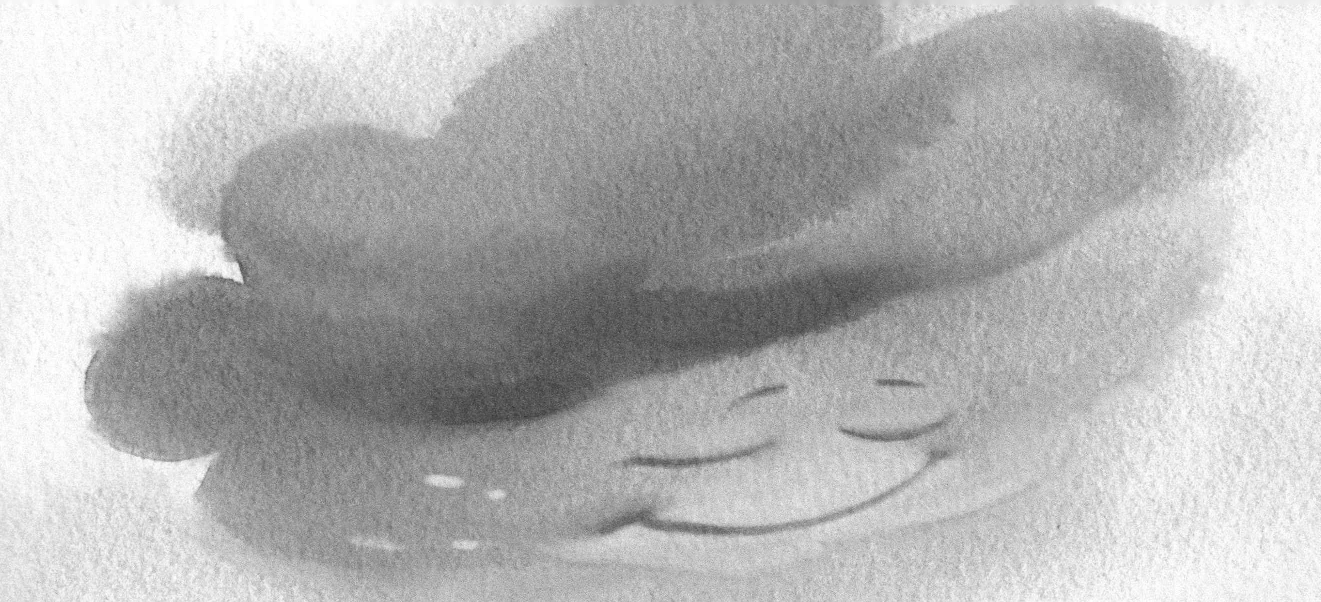

They were having so much fun that they lost track of time. It was time for bed.

"Good night, RC," said Scoot.

"See you in the morning," said Squawk.

RC was still not sure what to think about the very weird day he'd had. He floated above the forts wondering if he would wake up tomorrow and it would all be a dream. It had to be a dream because they hadn't told him he ruined things when he rained.

The next morning when RC woke up, the Go Aways were outside. He had definitely not been dreaming, so he asked them, “What is this place and why does the wind bring us here?”

“Well,” said Scoot, “we don’t know for sure but we think maybe the wind rescues us from the bullies and brings us here so we can have friends and not be yelled at all the time.”

“Maybe,” said Pip, “the wind knows we need to find a place where we are accepted for who we are.”

Squawk flew down and said to RC, “We like you for exactly who you are.”

“Yes,” said Scoot. “We had so much fun yesterday in your rain puddle.”

“We are glad you are here,” Potato said with a smile.

RC had that flutter again but now he knew this was what it felt like to be happy.

“Are there any more Go Aways?” asked RC.

Potato answered, “We have not seen any, but Pip hears noises sometimes in the night that the rest of us can’t. There used be flowers all around, but they began to disappear when the noises started.”

“We think they eat the flowers,” said Dilly, shaking.

“We call them the Night Creatures,” said Pip.

"Let's not talk about scary stuff anymore," said Potato. "It makes me scared."

"Me too," said Pip. "What do you want to do?"

"I know, let's play tumbleweed!" Dilly said.

All of a sudden RC called out from above, "Look, over there! I see a camel. Who is that?"

"Camels walk across the desert every now and then to take people from one place to another. They don't stay though," answered Scoot.

"It looks like something fell off the back of the camel," said RC. "Should we go see what it is?"

"Let's go!" said Scoot.

So, the six of them walked, flew, and floated over to see what had fallen off the camel.

As soon as they got close enough, Pip said, “It’s a flower.”

“We should take it home and plant it,” suggested Scoot.

So, Pip nestled the little flower into Potato’s quills, and they walked back home.

As soon as they got back to town, Scoot dug a hole. Pip gently took the flower out of Potato's quills, placed it in the hole and filled it back up with sand.

"There," said Dilly. "It will be okay here. Let's go play tumbleweed now."

"What is tumbleweed?" asked RC.

"It's a game we play. We roll ourselves up like a tumbleweed and roll really fast to see who gets to that cactus first," answered Squawk, pointing to a cactus in the distance.

"That sounds fun," said RC. "But I don't think I can roll myself into a ball on the ground. What can I do?"

"You can start the race, then float really fast to the cactus, to see who finishes first!" suggested Scoot.

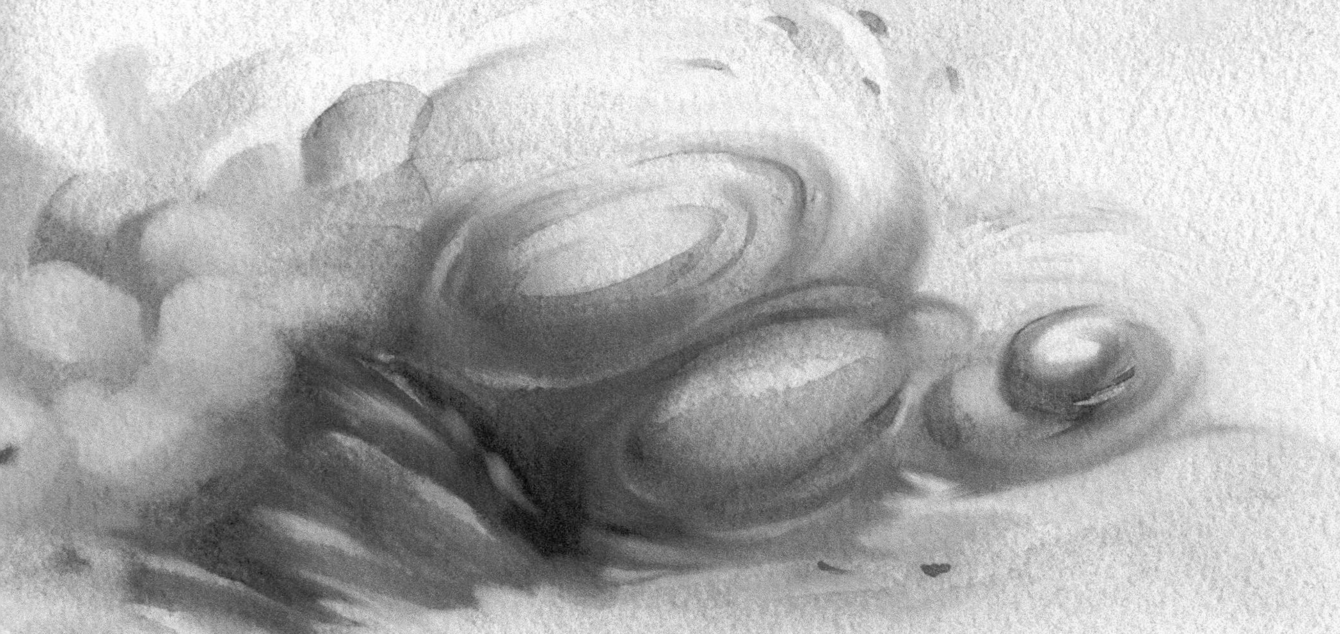

All the Go Aways lined up and RC started the race.

"One … two … three … go!" yelled RC.

Pip, Potato, Dilly, Scoot, and Squawk all rolled themselves into balls and rolled as fast as they could toward the cactus.

"Potato wins!" RC announced.

"Awesome job!" said Pip. "You rolled super-fast!"

Potato tried to say thank you, but his head was still spinning. All he could do was fall down.

They all laughed, all the way home as Potato tried to keep from falling down.

When they got to the town, they noticed that the flower was droopy.

"Oh no!" said Pip. "What happened to it?"

"Maybe it was out of the ground too long, riding on the camel," said Dilly. "Maybe watering it will help."

"We are in the GO AWAY desert. There isn't any water," Squawk said, very worried about their flower. "What will we do?"

None of the Go Aways knew what to do. They were incredibly sad.

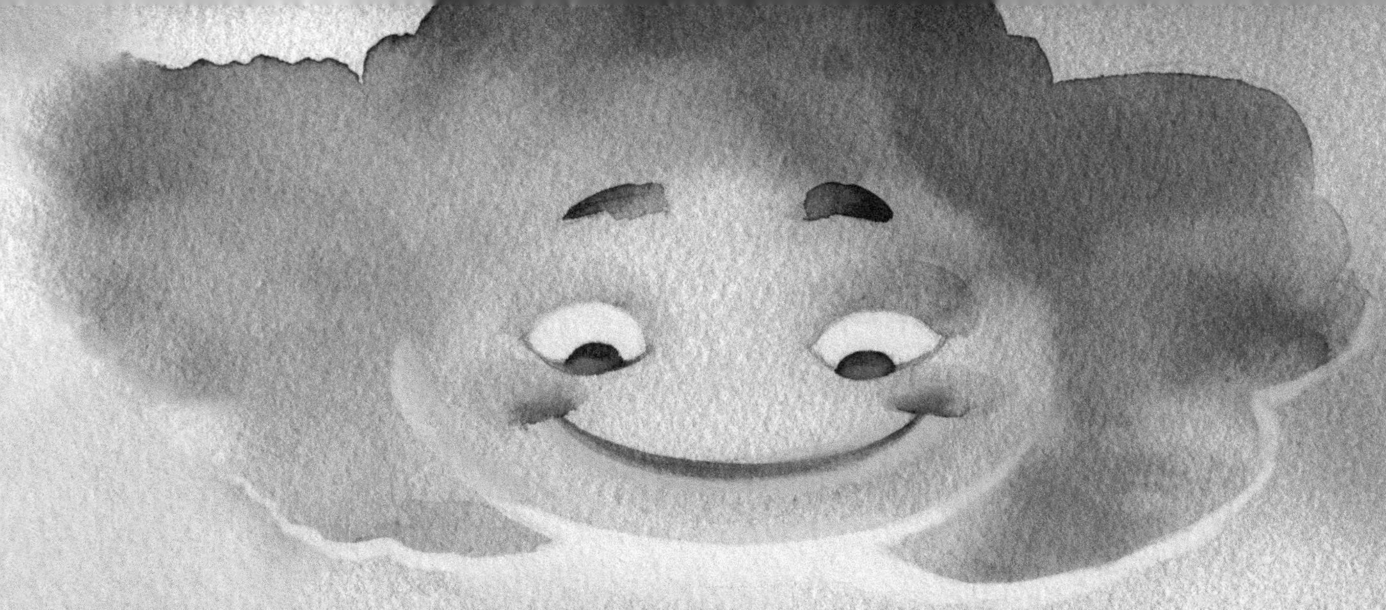

RC floated above the flower, then he turned himself into a watering can and rained. When he thought the flower had enough water, he turned back into himself.

All the Go Aways sat worried for a long time, watching the flower.

When it was almost dark, the flower sprang back to life.

"Oh look!" exclaimed Dilly. "RC, you saved the flower!"

They celebrated until the sun set, then they all said good night and went into their forts.

In the middle of the night, Pip ran out of her fort so scared. “Noises, I hear the noises again!”

Once everyone was outside and gathered around, Pip whispered, “They seem to be getting closer this time.”

“They have never come close before, why now?” asked Scoot, shaking

At the same time, they all looked over at the flower.

“I think they are coming to eat our flower,” said Squawk

“We can’t let them eat our flower,” said Scoot not quite as scared this time. “We need to protect it.”

As soon as the Night Creatures started to come towards the flower, RC rained on one of them. The Night Creature did not like getting wet and ran off.

Scoot ran toward one on his hind legs. His bright red color looked like fire and he scared away another.

Squawk flew straight at one and cawed. It was so loud the Night Creature ran off.

As another came towards the flower, Potato confronted it and opened all his eyes at the same time. The Night Creature took off.

Dilly watched as all his friends used their abilities to scare away the Night Creatures. "How can being slow help?" he thought out loud. Then he saw one of the Night Creatures coming towards him. He tried to run away, but he was too slow.

As the Night Creature caught up to Dilly, he heard it say, "We are trying to help!"

Dilly stopped and listened to the Night Creature.

Everyone was celebrating when Dilly walked back into town. But the celebrating stopped quickly when they noticed a Night Creature on Dilly's back.

"Dilly look out!" called RC. "You have one on your back. Hold on! I will scare him away!"

"*No!*" said Dilly. "They don't eat the flowers."

"Then what do they do with them?" asked RC.

"We take them home with us. These flowers are very unusual, so people come in on camels and take them. But, they are taking so many of them they will soon be extinct," answered the Night Creature.

"So, you are saving them, but why do you take them at night?" asked Potato.

"It's too hot during the day, so to protect their roots from the sun, we have to move them during the night, or they will become droopy and die," answered the Night Creature.

The Night Creature told them all about his home. It was an oasis with water and plants. It was surrounded by gigantic sand dunes so people would never find it.

After hearing all about the oasis, the Go Aways knew that this was where their flower belonged. As they followed the Night Creature to take the flower to its new home, RC realized that it doesn't matter if you are small like a flower, loud like Squawk or slow like Dilly, everyone belongs somewhere!

RC knew that he belonged here and that if you just look, you will find *your* somewhere place. It's even better if it's with a little help from others.

CPSIA information can be obtained
at www.ICGtesting.com
Printed in the USA
LVHW070733271020
669603LV00038B/342